Pig Man
and
Tin Dog

Written by
John Wood

Illustrated by
Jasmine Pointer

Can you say this sound and draw it with your finger?

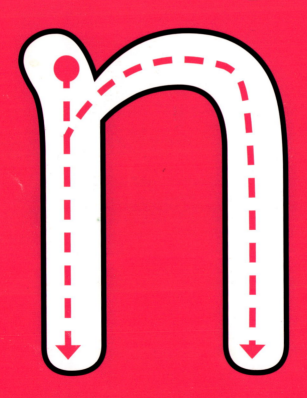

8121

Books should be returned or renewed by the last date above. Renew by phone **03000 41 31 31** or online *www.kent.gov.uk/libs*

Libraries Registration & Archives

Level 1 – Pink

Helpful Hints for Reading at Home

The graphemes (written letters) and phonemes (units of sound) used throughout this series are aligned with Letters and Sounds. This offers a consistent approach to learning whether reading at home or in the classroom.

HERE IS A LIST OF PHONEMES FOR THIS PHASE OF LEARNING. AN EXAMPLE OF THE PRONUNCIATION CAN BE FOUND IN BRACKETS.

Phase 2			
s (sat)	a (cat)	t (tap)	p (tap)
i (pin)	n (net)	m (man)	d (dog)
g (go)	o (sock)	c (cat)	k (kin)
ck (sack)	e (elf)	u (up)	r (rabbit)
h (hut)	b (ball)	f (fish)	ff (off)
l (lip)	ll (ball)	ss (hiss)	

HERE ARE SOME WORDS WHICH YOUR CHILD MAY FIND TRICKY.

Phase 2 Tricky Words			
the	to	I	no
go	into		

GPC focus: /i/n/m/d/g/o/c/

TOP TIPS FOR HELPING YOUR CHILD TO READ:

- Allow children time to break down unfamiliar words into units of sound and then encourage children to string these sounds together to create the word.

- Encourage your child to point out any focus phonics when they are used.

- Read through the book more than once to grow confidence.

- Ask simple questions about the text to assess understanding.

- Encourage children to use illustrations as prompts.

PHASE 2
/i/n/m/
d/g/o/
c/

This book focuses on the phonemes /i/, /n/, /m/, /d/, /g/, /o/ and /c/ and is a pink level 1 book band.

Pig Man

Written by
John Wood

Illustrated by
Jasmine Pointer

It is Pig Man.

Go, Pig Man, go!

Sit, Pig Man!

Pig Man in a gap.

Can Pig Man nap?

No nap, Pig Man.

Sip it, Pig Man!

Mop it, Pig Man!

Pig Man is on top.

Pig Man is not on top.

Can Pig Man nap?

Pig Man can nap.

Can you say this sound and draw it with your finger?

Tin Dog

Written by
John Wood

Illustrated by
Jasmine Pointer

It is a tin dog.

The tin dog is in!

Is it a dog?

It is a tin dog!

A dot on a dog.

No dot on a tin dog.

A pot and a pan?

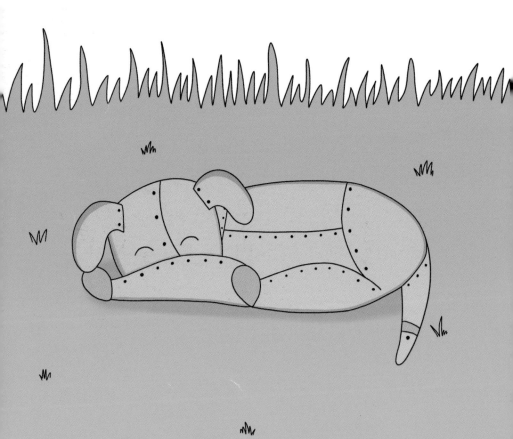

No. A tin dog.

A dog can nip.

Can a tin dog nip? No.

Pat the dog.

Pat the tin dog.

©2021 **BookLife Publishing Ltd.**
King's Lynn, Norfolk PE30 4LS

ISBN 978-1-83927-421-3

Pig Man & Tin Dog
Written by John Wood
Illustrated by Jasmine Pointer

An Introduction to BookLife Readers...

Our Readers have been specifically created in line with the London Institute of Education's approach to book banding and are phonetically decodable and ordered to support each phase of Letters and Sounds.

Each book has been created to provide the best possible reading and learning experience. Our aim is to share our love of books with children, providing both emerging readers and prolific page-turners with beautiful books that are guaranteed to provoke interest and learning, regardless of ability.

BOOK BAND GRADED using the Institute of Education's approach to levelling.

PHONETICALLY DECODABLE supporting each phase of Letters and Sounds.

EXERCISES AND QUESTIONS to offer reinforcement and to ascertain comprehension.

BEAUTIFULLY ILLUSTRATED to inspire and provoke engagement, providing a variety of styles for the reader to enjoy whilst reading through the series.

AUTHOR INSIGHT:
JOHN WOOD

An incredibly creative and talented author, John Wood has written about 60 books for BookLife Publishing. Born in Warwickshire, he graduated with a BA in English Literature and English Language from De Montfort University. During his studies, he learned about literature, styles of language, linguistic relativism, and psycholinguistics, which is the study of the effects of language on the brain. Thanks to his learnings, John successfully uses words that captivate and resonate with children and that will be sure to make them retain information. His stories are entertaining, memorable, and extremely fun to read.

PHASE 2

/i/n/m/
d/g/o/
c/

This book focuses on the phonemes /i/, /n/, /m/, /d/, /g/, /o/ and /c/ and is a pink level 1 book band.